BUZZING BEEHIVE!

by Christy Webster
illustrated by Alan Batson

A RANDOM HOUSE PICTUREBACK® BOOK

RANDOM HOUSE 🏠 NEW YORK

rhcbooks.com
minecraft.net
ISBN 978-0-593-90152-6 (trade) – ISBN 978-0-593-90153-3 (ebook)
Printed in the United States of America
10 9 8 7 6 5 4 3 2 1

On my latest adventure, I found a biome I'd never seen before—a cherry grove!

I was getting a closer look at the pink petals, when a cute little bee landed on the exact same flower.

I watched as the bee bumbled away, covered in pollen.

I followed the bee to see where it would go. It buzzed along until it reached a little nest on a nearby cherry tree.

I wondered if I could grab that nest and bring it home. Would the bees stay inside and come with me?

No! The moment I touched the nest, three angry bees popped out! I didn't wait to see what they would do next. I ran all the way home.

The next day, I was farming at my own base. To my surprise, another bee buzzed by! I kept very still as I watched.

I only had a few flowers in my garden, but the little bee stopped at each one before heading for the trees.

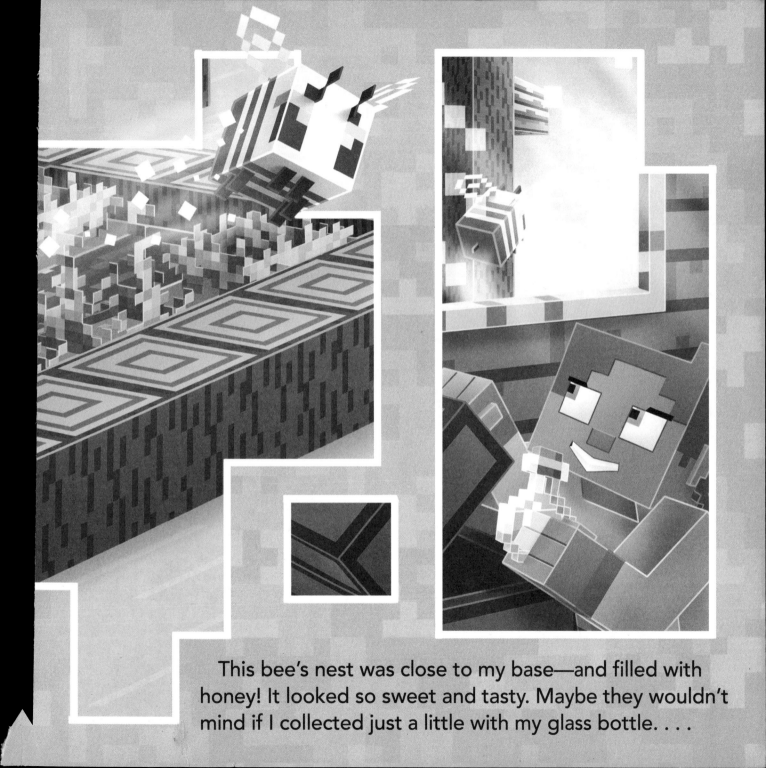

This bee's nest was close to my base—and filled with honey! It looked so sweet and tasty. Maybe they wouldn't mind if I collected just a little with my glass bottle. . . .

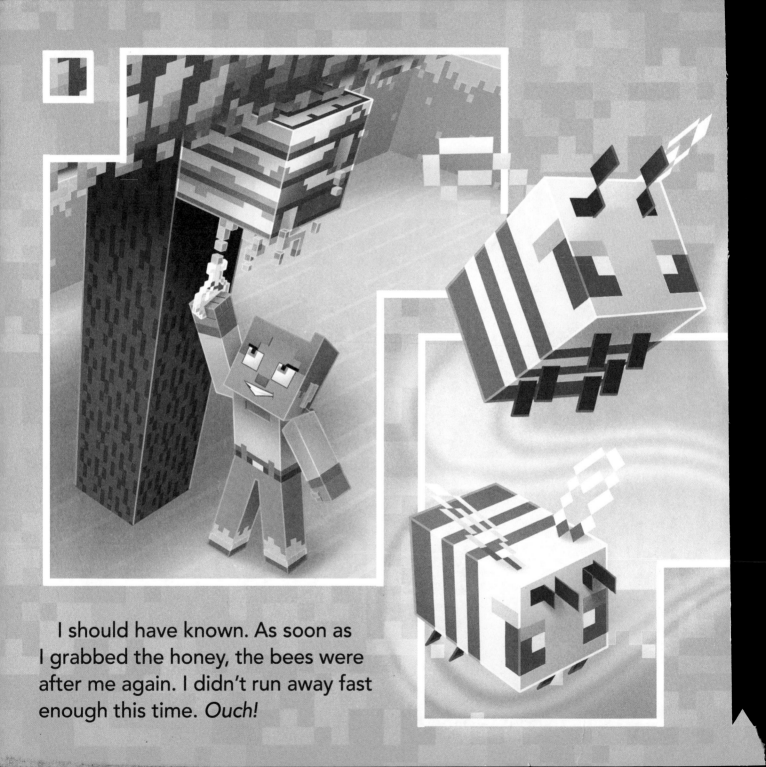

I should have known. As soon as
I grabbed the honey, the bees were
after me again. I didn't run away fast
enough this time. *Ouch!*

One of the bees stung me.

The bee sting gave me a poison effect. I could feel my health slipping away slowly.

All I had was the bottle of honey. I didn't know what else to do, so I drank it. I felt better right away. That was some good honey!

I continued watching the bees at a distance. I didn't want to get another sting. But that honey was so good I wanted to make friends with them!

Over my shoulder, I spotted my own campfire, puffing smoke into the sky. Would the smoke help calm the bees? Maybe . . .

Being very careful not to disturb the bees,
I built another campfire just under the nest.
The smoke started rising up and all around.
It was a relaxing sight.

I didn't take out my axe or a bottle this time. I pulled out my shears instead. The bees didn't get angry—and I got a whole honeycomb!

Back at my crafting table, I added string to the honeycomb to make pretty candles. I tried adding dye, and it worked! Now I could make candles in any color I wanted.

While I was making new discoveries, I noticed one of the bees buzz over my crops. I could see that it was carrying pollen. Suddenly, a patch of wheat grew faster!

Wow! So many good things happened after I made friends with the bees!
I got busy planting more flowers all around. Keeping the bees happy was my new mission!